This edition published by Parragon Books Ltd in 2014

Parragon Books Ltd
Chartist House
15–17 Trim Street
Bath BA1 1HA, UK
www.parragon.com

ISBN 978-1-4723-5654-3

Printed in China

Blooming Bows

Bath • New York • Cologne • Melbourne • Delhi
Hong Kong • Shenzhen • Singapore • Amsterdam

It's a busy day at Minnie's Bow-tique. Minnie and Daisy are getting ready for two special visitors.

"Daisy," says Minnie, "Have you found the camera?"

"Not yet," replies Daisy. "But I know it's here somewhere!"

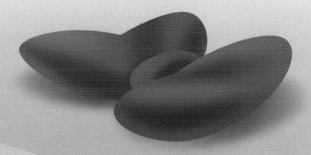

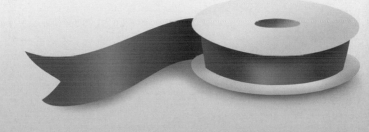

"Here it is, Daisy," says Minnie, pointing to Daisy's back. "Thanks!" says Daisy. "Now I'll be able to get a good picture of you with Millie and Melody."

Just then, Minnie hears giggling. "Get ready!" she cries. "Here they come!"

It's Minnie's twin nieces! They are wearing
their costumes for the Posy Pageant.

Daisy snaps some pictures of the twins. "Hold that pose, pretty posies!" Daisy says.

"Oh!" says Minnie. "You both look simply adorable!"

As the girls twirl round to show off their
costumes some of the flower petals fall off.
Cuckoo-Loca flies in to watch.

"All set for the Posy Pageant?" asks Cuckoo-Loca.

"We sure are, Cuckoo-Loca!" says Millie.
"Come on, Melody, let's show them our
posy-prance dance!"

But as the girls dance, the paper petals
fall to the floor....

"Is that supposed to happen?"
whispers Cuckoo-Loca, pointing to all of the
petals on the floor.

The girls start to sing:

"We can dance! We can sing!
On the first day of spring!
But you better make room,
'Cause it's time to bloom!"

When the twins stop singing and dancing, they notice all of their petals lying on the floor.

"That bloom went KA-BOOM!" says Cuckoo-Loca.

"Uh-oh," says Melody. "I guess the glue wasn't dry."

"I'll say," says Cuckoo-Loca.

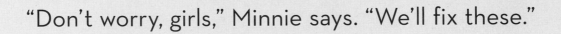
"Don't worry, girls," Minnie says. "We'll fix these."

"Oh, please be quick, Aunt Minnie!" says Melody.
"Or else we can't be in the pageant!" cries Millie.

"I've got the sticky-wicky goo-glue!" cries Daisy.

"Good thinking, Daisy!" says Minnie.

Minnie watches as Daisy glues the petals back on.
"Let's see, this pink one goes here, this purple one goes
there ... wait ... is that right?" asks Daisy.

"Daisy!" says Melody. "I'm Purple Posy!
Millie is Rosie Posy!"
Daisy has mixed up the colours.

Minnie gives the twins a big hug. "There, there, girls," she says. "I'll figure something out."

"But how?" asks Melody. "It's a flower
show, not a bow show!"

Suddenly Minnie has an idea. "Follow me!"
Grabbing an armful of fabric, Minnie leads Millie
and Melody to the dressing room.

While Minnie cuts fabric and ties ribbons, the twins giggle excitedly. Daisy and Cuckoo-Loca can't wait to see what Minnie is creating.

Soon, Minnie reappears. "Ladies and gentle-bird,
introducing our favourite flowers: Rosie Posy and Purple Posy!"

"Pop-up posies!" cries Daisy. "And no glue needed!"

"Now that's what I call getting out of a sticky situation,"
says Cuckoo-Loca.

Minnie gathers the twins. "Come on, my little posies. It's showtime!"

"Hey, girls!" Daisy calls, holding up her camera. "Say 'posies'!"

Millie and Melody wave goodbye as they
run out of the door.

"Wow, Minnie!" says Daisy, smiling at her friend.
"Who knew you had such flower power?"

"It's like I always say, Daisy," says Minnie,
"there's no business like bow business!"